Rocket Says
CLEAN UP!

Written by
Nathan Bryon

Illustrated by
Dapo Adeola

RANDOM HOUSE 🏠 NEW YORK

To my wonderful fiancée, Theresa; my incredible grandparents,
Ralph and Sylvia and Ann and Pat, who have always looked over me;
and Phaedra for keeping the Rocket energy alive daily! —N.B.

Dedicated to my ever-amazing nan, Rosaline Aderonke Tella,
who never lets me forget who I am—especially when it
feels like the rest of the world wants me to.
Love you like fried plantain. X —D.A.

Text copyright © 2020 by Nathan Bryon
Jacket art and interior illustrations copyright © 2020 by Dapo Adeola

All rights reserved. Published in the United States by Random House Children's Books, a division of Penguin Random House LLC, New York. Originally published in a slightly different form by Puffin Books, an imprint of Penguin Random House Children's Books UK, a division of Penguin Random House UK, London, in 2020.

Random House and the colophon are registered trademarks of Penguin Random House LLC.

Visit us on the Web! rhcbooks.com

Educators and librarians, for a variety of teaching tools, visit us at RHTeachersLibrarians.com

Library of Congress Cataloging-in-Publication Data is available upon request.
ISBN 978-0-593-11899-3 (trade) — ISBN 978-0-593-11900-6 (ebook)

MANUFACTURED IN CHINA
10 9 8 7 6 5 4 3 2 1
First American Edition

I can't sleep tonight.
I'm too excited!
Because tomorrow . . .

. . . me, my mom, and my big brother, Jamal, are going on vacation to see my grammy and grampy. It feels as though we've been packing **FOREVER**, but now we're ready to go!

I'm gonna be:

fist-bumping a turtle . . .

dancing with a dolphin . . .

high-fiving an octopus . . .

and surfing the
waves like awesome
Imani Wilmot.

DID YOU KNOW . . .
Imani Wilmot created
the first female surf
competition in Jamaica?

As soon as we arrive, I give my
grammy and grampy a **HUGE** hug.

My grandparents are the best. They run whale-watching tours and have an animal sanctuary behind their house.

I can't wait to help!

Grampy tells me we never touch wild animals
unless they need to be rescued or cared for.

But first it's time to surf!
My grammy is really good!

Then Mom and I build a **HUGE** sandcastle!

OH NO! A baby turtle has washed up
onshore, all tangled in plastic.

I pick her up gently and take
her to Grammy and Grampy—
they can fix this.

Grammy says she will
try her best, and takes
her back to the sanctuary.

"Plastic is ruining these islands, Rocket," says Grampy sadly.

"We save as many creatures as we can, but some stay away. People used to come here to see the whales, but we haven't spotted a whale in a long time."

He leads me down the beach.

It feels as though there is more plastic than there is sand!

I feel really sad. We need to **DO** something. But what?

The next day at the beach, there are people playing in the sand, swimming in the sea, and eating Popsicles, but all I notice now is the plastic.

Surely they see it too?

I need to let **EVERYONE** know!

DID YOU KNOW . . . whales eat the plastic and it makes them sick?

DID YOU KNOW . . . nearly half the trash in the sea comes directly from careless people?

DID YOU KNOW . . . there are over 5.25 TRILLION pieces of plastic in the ocean?

Soon we have lots of new friends who want to help.

As the day goes on, more and more people join.
We spend the whole day cleaning the beach.

Even Jamal helps!

The **CLEANUP CREW** is amazing!

And soon the beach is . . .

CLE

AN!

But now what do we do with all the plastic we collected?

Theresa, part of the **CLEANUP CREW**, has a brilliant idea.

"My mom is an artist—maybe we could
get her to create something out of it!"

YESSSSS!

Theresa's mom makes awesome bins for trash . . .
out of the trash we collected!

And the **CLEANUP CREW** makes
the front page of the newspaper
and the TV news!

Island News

Clean Beach

Now no one will forget why we need to **CLEAN UP!**

Everyone on the island wants clean beaches.

Everyone on the island wants clean water.

Everyone on the island wants to bring back the whales.

The next day, Grammy and Grampy have a BBQ for the whole **CLEANUP CREW**. The smell of Grammy's special sauce wafts around the island.

And best of all, while everyone's talking and laughing and eating, Grampy and I release the turtle we rescued back into the sea and watch as she swims away.

She's all better now!

And I just know one day the whales will come back!

DID YOU KNOW . . . one day you are going to change the world, Rocket?

Here's how **YOU** can help clean up the beaches!

REDUCE the plastic you use by switching to reusable water bottles, bringing your own bags to the grocery store, and avoiding plastic straws and utensils.

GO ORGANIC with your sunscreen. Lots of the chemicals in sunscreens that aren't organic can harm wildlife when they wash off your skin and into the ocean.

DISPOSE of your trash properly. Separate it carefully for recycling. Rinse plastic things so they can be processed by recycling plants.

For more information on why plastic in the ocean is such a problem, and what else *else* YOU can do to fix it,
visit: montereybayaquarium.org/conservation-and
-science/our-priorities/ocean-plastic-pollution

Have your grown-ups visit:
plasticpollutioncoalition.org